ITEMS OF

HIVE TOOL
for levering open
parts of hive

SMOKER

UNCAPPING
KNIFE
for removing
wax capping
from honeycomb

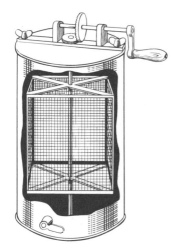

HONEY EXTRACTOR
Honeycomb is revolved
rapidly to throw honey
onto the sides of the drum

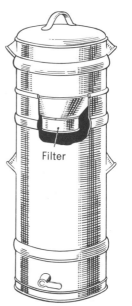

Filter

HONEY TANK

Man has used honey as a sweetener since earliest times, and there are many references to it in ancient literature — as well as many myths and errors concerning the life of the honey-bee.

We know the honey-bee to be not only a honey producer, but also one of the most important insect pollinators of both crop plants and wild flowers. Without it, many crops could not be grown economically. Today, as never before, the honey-bee faces the danger of careless spraying of insecticides and weedkillers on plants in bloom. Protection of the honey-bee against these risks is essential for future crop production even more than for honey production.

This book tells of the marvellously efficient and highly organized life of the honey-bee, from the laying of the eggs by the queen, the growth of the larvae, the contribution of the 'drones' and the 'workers', to the swarming of an over-populated colony and the handling of bees by the modern bee-keeper.

life of the
Honey-bee

by W. SINCLAIR, Ph. D.

with illustrations by JILL PAYNE

Ladybird Books Loughborough

The honey-bee

The honey-bee has been known to man for many thousands of years. A very old rock-painting in Spain shows the removal of honey from a nest of wild bees.

Four kinds of honey-bee exist in the world, but in Britain we have only one, the Western Honey-bee, of which there are several different forms, all very closely related. They differ in their colours, a little in size, and in the length of their tongues. Some work in poorer weather than others, some eat more than others, but all of them produce honey, and this is why we are interested in them.

Honey is a very good food for everyone. It is especially good for people who are ill, as it gives energy quickly and is the food most easily absorbed by the human body.

Bees live in hives. The man who looks after them is the bee-keeper, and his group of hives is called an apiary. All the honey-bees, even in an apiary, are really wild animals and have not been tamed in the same way as horses and cattle. Very occasionally bees make their home in the open, hanging their combs from branches as shown in the picture. But such a colony cannot survive winter rain.

Let us have a closer look at this remarkable insect, the honey-bee.

A natural colony of bees and comb in a thorn hedge. Cold and rain would eliminate such a colony in Britain

What the honey-bee looks like

In some ways the honey-bee resembles many other insects. It has a head, a thorax carrying the wings and legs and an abdomen which is more than half the length of the whole bee.

But let us look more closely. The head has two big, many sided, compound eyes, one on each side. There are three much smaller simple eyes on the very top of the head. From the front of the face come two long feelers or antennae, with which the bee can sense touch, taste and smell. On the bottom of the head is the sucking tongue which the bee uses for taking up its food and for ripening nectar. It is folded away when not in use. The mandibles are used for working wax.

The thorax carries the wings. You will see that the front pair is bigger than the hind pair and the two wings of each side are hooked together. The three pairs of legs have many special structures. The back legs have brushes for cleaning pollen off the body, and a basket in which pollen can be carried back to the hive. Each front leg has a very small notch, lined with hairs, which is used for cleaning the antennae.

At the tip of the abdomen is the weapon we all respect, the sting!

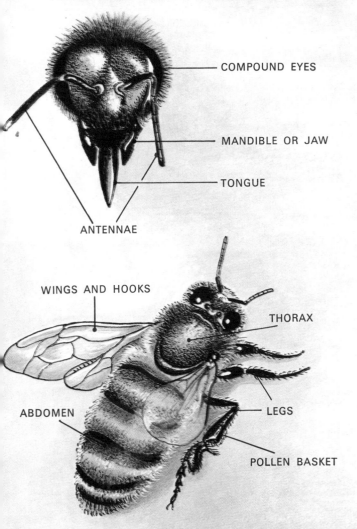

FRONT VIEW OF HEAD

COMPOUND EYES

MANDIBLE OR JAW

TONGUE

ANTENNAE

WINGS AND HOOKS

THORAX

ABDOMEN

LEGS

POLLEN BASKET

A year in the hive

You do not expect to find bees in your garden in the middle of winter. The flowers, where the bee finds its food, are present only in the warmer times of the year, so it is during the spring and summer that the bees are out and about. As the summer approaches, more and more bees are raised, until the greatest number is present in the hives about the middle of June. This large number is kept up until about August, when the number drops off again. All this time the bees fly out, whenever the weather is good enough, to collect food from the flowers.

As the days become colder, the bees stay in the hive and cluster on the combs to keep themselves warm. They do not sleep through the winter as the dormice do. All through winter they eat their stores of honey to keep themselves alive. As the warm days of spring come round the bees venture out again.

But, you might say, you have seen bees flying near their hives on a mild day in the middle of winter. They do fly on very good days, and the reason is that they go out to empty their bowels, as they will not soil the hive if it is possible to avoid this. Sometimes the sun shining on snow tempts the bees out as if it were a summer day, and when this happens many bees are caught in the cold and die.

1. Winter. Bees stay in the hive
2. Spring. Bees venture out to find early flowers
3. Summer. Many bees to many flowers. Honey stored in top part of hive
4. Autumn. Few bees flying. Honey removed for sale

1,

2,

3,

4,

The worker bees

Of the three types of bee in a hive, worker bees are the ones you are most likely to see. They are the ones which go out to the flowers to gather nectar and pollen. They are females by nature, but cannot lay eggs except in very unusual circumstances. Their work is caring for the eggs and larvae in the hives, building combs, feeding the queen bee and keeping her spick and span, guarding the hive against intruders and searching for nectar and pollen from many kinds of flowers. The life of the worker bees can be very short, only four to five weeks in the height of the summer when they are doing a great deal of flying. But the workers which survive winter may live for more than six months.

The worker is the smallest of the three types of honeybee in the colony, but workers make up for their small size by numbering about 98% of the bees in the colony. They can, of course, sting. They do this only when the colony seems to be in need of defence, or if they are trapped: if you hold them in your hand, for example. After stinging a human being, a bee usually dies. This is because it cannot pull out the sting from our flesh: in attempting to do so, the sting is torn from its own body.

A worker bee gathers nectar and pollen

The queen bee

There is only one queen bee in a hive, unless the circumstances are unusual. She is bigger than the other bees, having a long abdomen. Her wings appear rather short, but in fact they are slightly longer than those of the workers. Her thorax is broader than that of the worker bee. Her legs are brighter in colour, and somewhat orange-brown. Very often she looks smoother and shinier than other bees, and moves among them quite slowly and 'majestically'. She can live for three years or more.

The queen is the only bee that can lay eggs which will produce worker bees or more queens. In fact, this is the only task she has. The workers feed and clean her, so that she can spend as much as possible of her time laying the precious eggs. She is fed with special food from glands in the heads of the workers. This helps her to lay up to 2,000 eggs per day. She flies only on her wedding flight and when the colony swarms.

Like the worker bee, the queen has a sting, but it is curved, unlike the straight sting of the worker. She is unlikely to use it against human beings, but keeps it almost entirely for use against rival queens, as you will read later in this book.

A queen bee and her 'court'

The male or drone bees

Drones are the true males, a few of which will be the queen's wedding partners. They are present only from about the beginning of May until perhaps September. They are heavily built, squat, very hairy and often appear slow and lazy. Even their low droning noise in flight, which gives them their name, sounds sleepy. They cannot go out for nectar for themselves, but get all their food from the workers or sometimes take it straight from the honey cells in the honeycombs.

They fly only on days when the sun is very warm, usually in the early afternoon. Unlike the workers, they can come and go from hive to hive without difficulty, but they usually stay with the hive where they were hatched.

At the end of summer they are dragged out of the hive by the workers and left to die of hunger and cold. Since they eat so much, they would be a heavy burden on the winter food store if they were allowed to spend the winter in the hive. To us it seems a cruel fate, but bees work only on the basis of efficiency, and do not tolerate useless drones when times are hard.

A worker bee feeds a drone (right)

The honeycombs

In the hive, bees build combs where they raise young and store food. The combs are made of beeswax. Wild bees use only the wax they produce from their own bodies, and their natural combs may be quite long. Bee-keepers help the bees by giving them frames made of wood which hold sheets of salvaged beeswax with the pattern of the cells already pressed in. These combs are about 35 to 45 cms. long by 15 to 30 cms. deep. The bees build up this foundation and make combs very quickly.

The combs are made of six-sided cells, with the closed bottoms of the cells back to back, so that each comb is really two cells thick. The cells have the mouth slightly higher than the base, which helps to prevent the honey running out.

There are two main types of cell: the smaller ones, in which worker bees are raised from the egg, are about five millimetres across; the larger cells, in which the drones are raised, are about seven millimetres across and deeper.

Both these types of cell can be used for honey storage. A 35 cms. by 22 cms. comb holds about three kilogrammes of honey when full.

There is a third type of cell, the queen cell, but this is not part of the comb in the usual sense. You can read more about queen cells on page 22.

1. A magnified cross-section showing cells and mouths of cells
2. A comb

16

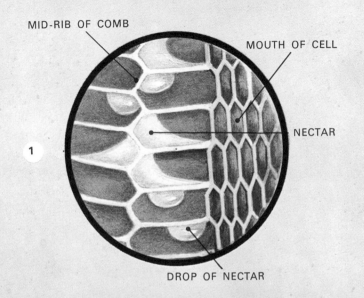

MID-RIB OF COMB

MOUTH OF CELL

NECTAR

DROP OF NECTAR

1

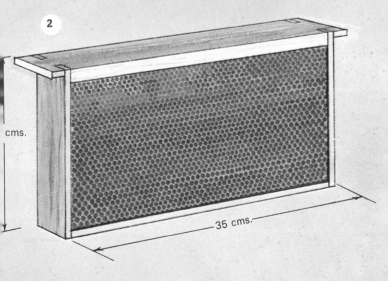

2

cms.

35 cms.

Beeswax

Bees produce beeswax from their own bodies. On the underside of their abdomens they have four pairs of glands, the wax glands. They pass the wax out as little flakes or scales from these glands. Under the wax glands are tiny pockets which hold the wax scales as they are being made. When a wax scale is ready for use, the bee takes it out of the wax pocket by spiking it on the strong hairs of its back legs, and then passes it to the jaws. There it is chewed, and other materials may be mixed with the wax. When it is soft, the worker bee puts it into place on the comb being built. You will see that it takes many, many wax scales to make even one honeycomb.

Wax can be made only if the worker bees are very warm. To get this warmth they cluster together on the comb they are building. Usually workers about ten to sixteen days old do the work, but older bees can do it if necessary in any emergency.

Since bees need about five kilogrammes of sugar to make half a kilogramme of wax, it is easy to understand why the beekeeper saves all his scraps of wax. He melts them down and purifies them, and has them rolled out into sheets of clean, new, comb foundation. The bees use this as a starting material, and are saved a considerable amount of work, time and energy. The bee-keeper gains by getting more honey.

1. Wax scales being produced from the bee's body
2. Spiked scale being passed to jaws

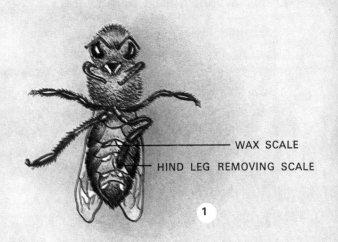

WAX SCALE

HIND LEG REMOVING SCALE

1

SCALE SPIKED
ON HAIRS OF BACK LEG

2

Eggs, larvae, pupae and adults

Like other insects, bees are produced from eggs. The eggs of the bee are laid only by the queen. She lays one in each cell of the comb, working out from the centre. She can lay up to 2,000 eggs each day when she is working hardest. If she lays an egg in a worker cell, this egg will produce a worker larva, which will eventually change into a worker bee. If the egg is in a drone cell, it will produce a male or drone bee. If it is in a queen cell, it will produce a queen.

The eggs are very small, just big enough to see with the naked eye. After three days, the tiny larva hatches from each egg. It is fed for three days on food from the head glands of the workers. It grows rapidly, and you can then see that it is white and wormlike in shape. For another two days it is fed pollen and nectar. Then, five days after hatching, the worker larva has its cell capped or covered over by the adult worker bees nursing it. In its sealed cell it changes into a pupa. This is a little more like the adult bee, but is still whitish.

After 21 days, when it is fully grown, the young worker has changed into an adult bee. It chews through the cap over its cell and crawls out onto the comb. At this stage it is still rather slow and looks very fluffy, but it is soon able to run over the combs like older bees.

1. Eggs in cells (magnified)
2. Cells with larvae of various ages
3. Worker larvae change into pupae
4. After 21 days—a fully grown worker bee

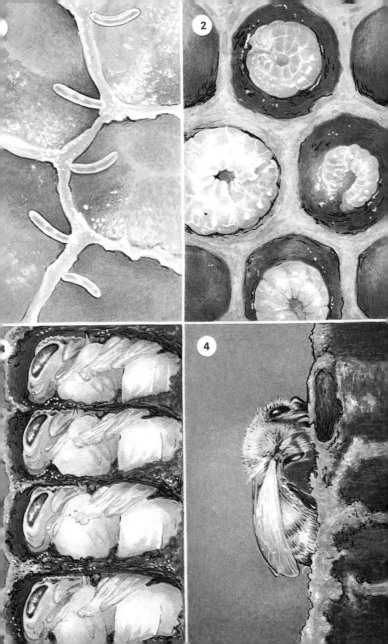

The queen cell

The queen cell is a very special cell for a very special bee! Usually only a few are built each year, and sometimes none at all. If the bees are going to swarm (see page 28), you might find about a dozen queen cells. If they are raising a new queen to replace or supersede the old one, the bees will make even fewer, perhaps only two or three, queen cells.

The queen cell is unlike the ordinary cells of the comb in that it is used once only. Instead of lying flat, it has its mouth pointing straight downwards. It is a big cell, about 2.5 cms. long, more or less round instead of six-sided, and looks like a large, dimpled acorn. It is made of wax, like the other cells, but usually has a lot of pollen mixed in with the wax. This gives the queen cell a darker colour than a newly-made worker or drone cell.

The queen cell starts as a little queen cup, and as the young queen larva inside grows, the cell is built up by the workers until it reaches its full size. Then it is sealed over, or capped, until the queen is ready to come out, fifteen to sixteen days after the egg was laid. She chews away the rim of the cap, and pushes it off like a hinged lid. Then she can crawl out.

When the queen has come out, the workers soon tear down the empty queen cell.

Queen cells—with a queen emerging from one

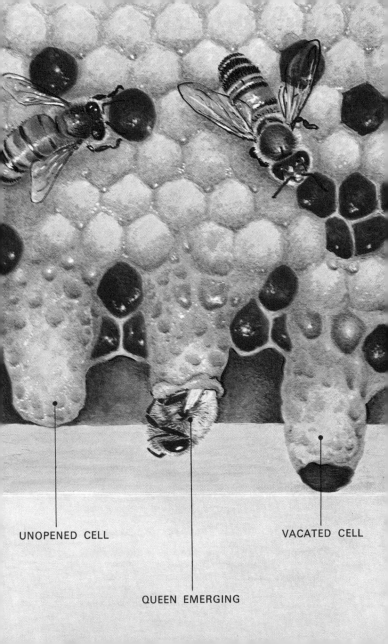

UNOPENED CELL

VACATED CELL

QUEEN EMERGING

The queen is lost!

Since the queen is the only bee in the hive that can lay eggs, the colony is in difficulties if she is lost. As soon as a queen is lost, the bees raise a new one. How? Any worker larva which is not over three days old can be changed to a queen if it is fed the correct food. Instead of having the special food from the head glands of the nursing workers *for only the first three days of its life*, it is fed with this food all through its larval life of five days. The cell it is in is enlarged by the workers, and looks like a proper queen cell.

By this treatment, the bees are able to change the larva from that of a worker to that of a queen. After coming out of her cell and taking her wedding flight, this new queen is able to carry on just like the one which was lost. The older the larva chosen to have this special treatment, the less efficient she will be as a queen. She can still lay eggs, from which the bees can raise a new queen to replace her, if need be. The bees do not raise only one queen, of course; they raise several if the old queen is lost. Only one is allowed finally to become the laying queen.

How can a queen get lost? A little mistake by the bee-keeper might kill her, or she might die from disease.

Emergency queen cells after the loss of a queen

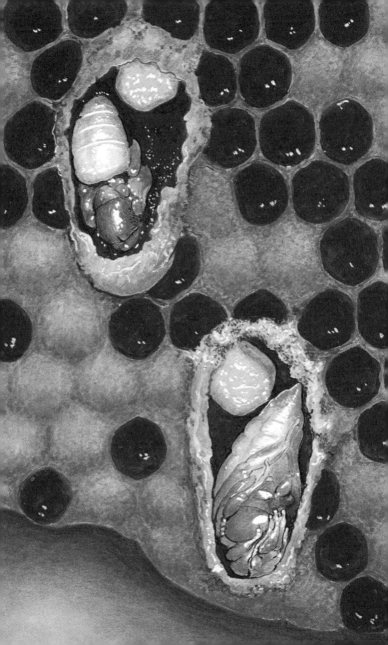

The wedding flight of the queen

When a queen is young, she has to meet a husband. Although many males are present in the hive, she will have nothing to do with them there. Instead she leaves the hive and soars up into the air, with the males from her own hive following her, and males from nearby hives as well. On this flight she is a strong flier, and only the strongest and fittest drones will catch her. This helps to make sure that only the strongest bees will be raised from these parents.

As she flies up, the males chase her, and eventually one or more catch her and mating takes place. It used to be thought that only one drone mated with the queen, but recent research suggests that up to ten drones may mate with the queen. When this wedding flight is over, the queen comes back to the hive and settles down to laying eggs for the rest of her life. She will stop laying for a short time and fly again only if the colony swarms.

This wedding flight occurs when the adult queen is about a week old, if the weather is good enough. It can happen only on a fine, sunny day, and bad weather can stop it very easily. If the flight is delayed by bad weather for too long, the queen will probably never make her flight and is then useless. The bee-keeper has to remove her and give the colony a new queen.

The wedding flight of a queen—with drones in pursuit

The swarm

Since only the queen can lay eggs, any new colony must have a queen. A few workers on their own cannot found a new colony.

When a colony gets very strong in numbers, there is every chance it will swarm. It starts preparing for this early in the season, by producing drones and queens. When the new queens in their cells are just capped over, and therefore safe, the old queen and about half the workers and many of the drones in the colony fly out together. Since they may number 30,000 or more, it is an awesome sight. This mass of bees is the 'swarm'. The whole swarm usually alights on a nearby tree branch or hedge after coming out of the hive. After a time, it takes to the air again, flies off to its new home and settles in. Workers draw out combs, and the queen lays in them. So the new colony gets its queen by taking her with them.

But what of the old colony? Soon, one or more of its young queens comes out of her cell. She may kill all the other queens, or she may take off with another smaller swarm or cast. Eventually, one queen is left in the hive; she takes her wedding flight, and life in the hive goes back to normal.

A swarm of bees on a branch

What bees do in the hive

After coming out of her cell, a young worker bee spends the first three days cleaning cells in which the queen will eventually lay. She is also gaining strength for harder work. From the fourth to the ninth day she is a nurse bee. She produces brood food from the glands in her head, and feeds it to the younger larvae. She also makes up a mixture of honey and pollen, the bee bread, and feeds it to the older larvae.

By the ninth day her head glands have reached the end of their normal working, and the wax glands on her abdomen have become active. Therefore, from the tenth to the sixteenth day the worker builds comb, using her wax for this purpose. At the end of this time the wax glands finish their activity. Then the bee spends from the seventeenth to the nineteenth day accepting pollen and nectar from the field bees, and storing it in the cells. She helps to ripen the nectar, and presses the pollen down into the cells for storage.

On the twentieth day some bees act as guards, standing at the door keeping out bees from other colonies and arresting other strangers which are not allowed into the hive. From the twenty-first day until the end of her life, she will work in the fields, looking for and bringing home pollen and nectar.

Although this is her typical time-table, it can be altered whenever changes are necessary. Even old bees can build comb and feed larvae if the need is urgent.

1. Nurse bees feeding larvae
2. Worker bees packing pollen in the cells
3. Worker bees storing nectar
4. Guard bees arresting a stranger

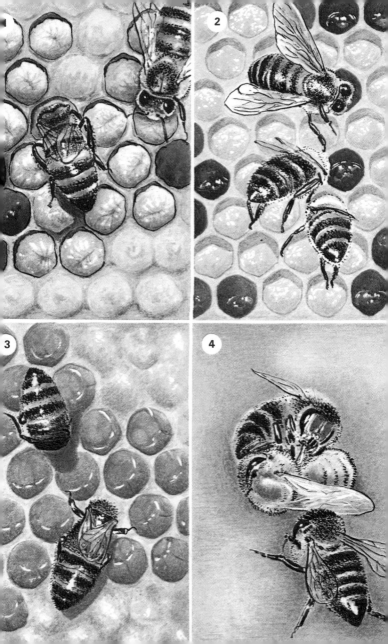

Nectar and pollen

The bees you see flying among the flowers are seeking two things from the plants—nectar and pollen. Nectar is the sweet liquid which plants produce to attract insects for pollination. It consists of sugars dissolved in water. Most of this sugar is the same as the cane sugar we put in our tea and coffee. Different plants have nectars with more or less sugar, and the bees prefer the strongest nectars. They suck up the sugary liquid from the nectaries of the flower, and store it in their honey stomach to carry it back to the hive. There, they pass it on to the hive bees, which change the cane sugar to simpler sugars, reduce the amount of water in the nectar, and then store it in the cells as honey for use as needed.

Pollen is the fine, dusty material you see on the stamens of flowers. It is black in the poppy, yellow in the dandelion, and so on. Bees get this pollen on their bodies as they search for the nectar in the flowers. They clean off the pollen with their legs, and store it in the special pollen baskets on the outside surface of the hind legs ready to be carried back to the hive. There they put it into the pollen storage cells where it is packed down by hive bees which use their heads as hammers. Pollen is stored near the larvae, so that it is easily available when feeding the young—who will eat most of it.

Worker bees gathering nectar and pollen

How bees use nectar and pollen

Nectar can be used immediately to feed bees and young in the hive. It is one of the foods essential to the bee. If it is not used at once, the bees store the changed nectar as honey, for use later on. If they have more than they need, the bee-keeper removes the surplus honey for his own use. The honey used by the bees in their food has the same value to them as bread, sugar, syrup and such things have to us.

Pollen is to the bee what meat, fish, sausages and similar foods are to human beings. It gives them protein, which is the name of a group of chemicals needed for building muscles and other flesh in the bee's body. Without this important material, the bees cannot grow properly.

The young larvae are not fed directly with pollen. Instead, the worker bees use pollen to produce a special food from glands in the head. This food is easier for the young larvae to take in, just as we feed human babies on specially prepared foods. Later on, the bees give the larvae a mixture of honey and pollen, called bee bread, which the larvae are then able to eat directly.

The extra pollen needed for winter is stored in cells under a layer of honey, which preserves it from going bad.

Worker bees exchanging food

Nectar ripening

When nectar is brought in from the flowers, it contains too much water to be safely stored. It has to have a lot of the water removed from it before it will keep. This work is one of the tasks of the hive bees. First of all the nectar may be stored in cells where it can await attention. When it is to be ripened, the worker bees take a drop into their stomachs, and then go to a quiet place on the comb. There they draw out the drop on the tongue, exposing the nectar to the air, so that water is lost. After about twenty seconds, the drop is drawn back into the bee, and put out again. This goes on time after time, until the nectar has lost most of its water.

At the same time as the bees are removing the water, they are changing the sugars in the nectar so that it becomes honey.

Now the honey can be put into the cells, where a little further ripening takes place. When this is complete, the honey cell is capped over with wax, and the honey is safe for a long time. It is also ready for us to enjoy.

1. Bee ripening nectar on her tongue
2. Bee packing honey in cell

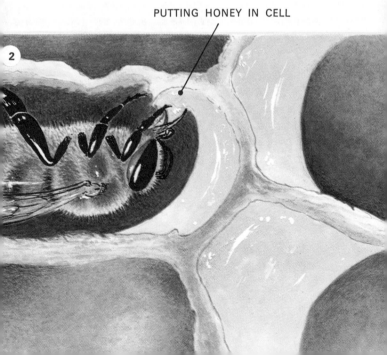

DROP OF NECTAR ON TONGUE

PUTTING HONEY IN CELL

Propolis: bee glue

Bees gather a sticky material from the buds of various plants, such as the chestnut, and carry it home to the hive. It is not a food but a building material called propolis or bee-glue. They use it to 'cement' together everything in the hive, and to fill up any chinks in the hive which might let in water or wind. They gather it by packing it into their pollen baskets and carrying it home in this way. In the hive they have to get the help of other bees to remove it, as it is difficult for them to handle it by themselves.

As well as using propolis as a cement, the bees are said to use it in very small amounts in the construction of combs, to give added strength.

Bees are very clean animals and will allow nothing smelly or rotten in the hive. Sometimes a mouse or a big beetle gets into the hive and dies there. Since it is too big for the bees to drag out, they can deal with it only by wrapping it up. They do this by completely sealing the dead animal in a coating of propolis. This prevents the mouse rotting and making a nasty smell. The propolis preserves the dead flesh rather like the way Egyptian mummies were preserved.

A bee collecting propolis or 'bee glue' from horse-chestnut

Finding the way

If we want to find out how to get somewhere we can use a map. How do the bees navigate? From about the tenth day of her life a worker bee takes short flights in front of the hive. She is learning its position and the landmarks near it, so that she can find her way back to it. She does this so well that if you move the hive when she is out she will keep flying around in the same area where the hive used to be. She cannot recognise the hive as such, only its position, so that even if the hive were only a few metres away, and in full view, she would not find it.

The older she gets, the further the worker will fly. When searching for food she may fly several kilometres from the hive. How does she find her way now? Her compass is the sun and the pattern of light in the sky. But the sun appears to move as the day passes. It rises in the east and sets in the west. The bee can allow for this passage of time and movement of the sun, and it does not upset her compass in the least. Not only can the bee use this sun compass, but she can tell other bees how to navigate by it to reach places where she has found food.

Above: Man's magnetic compass and the bee's sun compass
Below: Bees can follow a sun compass direction to find flowers

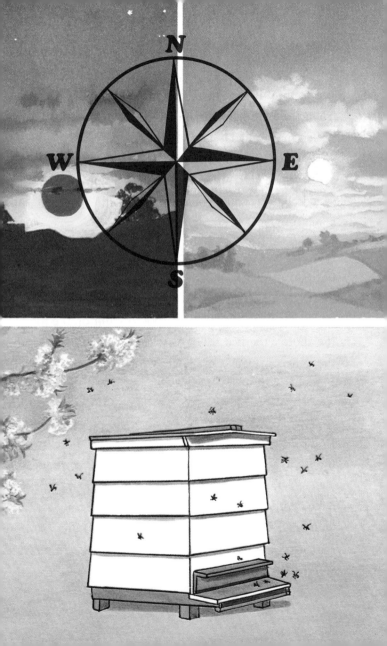

The bees' language

When a worker bee finds a good source of food it is very helpful if she can tell other bees in her hive about it. Then they can help her to gather the crop of nectar or pollen more quickly and while it is available. How can we test to see whether this can be done? Let us put some syrup made with water and ordinary cane sugar into a saucer. Put the saucer on the window-sill of a house near some beehives.

It might take some hours or even days for one bee to find it. But very soon after she has found it we see many more bees coming along to have some of the food. If we were able to mark with a spot of paint on the top of the thorax the bee which first came there, and also all the others which came later, we would soon see that they all came from the same hive. In time, of course, bees from other hives might also discover the food.

Since the bees suddenly appear after the discovery of the food by one bee, does she tell her sisters about it? Yes, she does. How? By doing one of two main types of dance in the hive, on the vertical face of the combs. The dances have been seen for many years but Professor von Frisch of Bavaria, in Germany, was the first to understand their meaning.

Bees find a saucer of syrup

The round dance and the waggle dance

The Round Dance is used when the food source is *less* than 100 metres from the hive. The dancing bee runs round in a circle on the comb, turns round and does the same circle in the opposite direction and so on. Other workers near her on the comb follow her movements with their antennae, and run after her.

During the dance, as at other times, the bees exchange food. In this way, the dancing bee gives the others a taste of the food she has found, and also some of its perfume.

Dishes placed at the same distance from the hive, but in different directions, seem to attract about the same number of bees at each. So the Round Dance tells the bees—'There is food within a distance of 100 metres, and it has this taste and smell'.

The Waggle Dance is used when the food is *more* than 100 metres away. The dancing bee runs in one direction, waggling her body very quickly from side to side. She then turns round and runs in a semi-circle back to the starting point, repeating the performance again and again, sometimes returning along the opposite semi-circle. The fewer times this dance is done in a certain period, the further the food is from the hive, and the other bees can judge the distance. When the waggle run is straight up the comb, the food lies in the direction of the sun. When straight down, the food is directly opposite the sun's direction from the hive, and when the waggle is at an angle, this tells the bees the angle to fly from the direction of the sun. The Waggle Dance, therefore, tells both the sun-compass direction to fly, and how far. The taste and smell of the food tells what to search for. The longer the dance lasts, the stronger the food source.

Above: Round Dance. Below: Waggle Dance

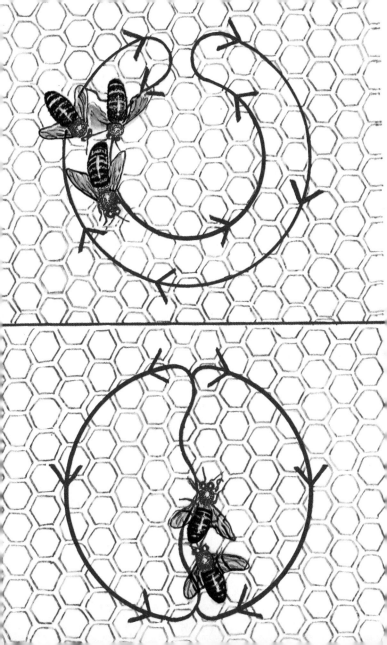

How the bees find a new home

The bees of the swarm cluster have to find a new home in which to live. And they must all agree where this is to be. How do they do this?

The dances used are the same as those for telling each other about food sources. Those 'scout' bees which are out looking for a new home, perhaps in a hole in a tree or in a wall, come back to the swarm cluster, and dance on it to tell the other bees about their find. If it is a good home, they dance more enthusiastically than they do if it is a poor home. Bees which have found a poor home in their searches will go out to inspect the homes found by others, and dance for the new and better one when they return.

Gradually, all the bees looking for a home agree that one particular site is the best, and only when they do agree will they all fly off to take possession of it. They go directly in the 'bee-line' we talk about.

When they are judging their new homes, bees take account of many factors; they prefer sheltered to exposed homes, dry ones to wet ones, etc. They will refuse to occupy a home which is likely to be invaded by ants, or is likely to be flooded if there is heavy rain.

Bees in a swarm cluster decide on a new home

Water

Bees obtain a large amount of water in the nectars they gather during the year, but sometimes this is not enough. In spring the bees feed on the very strong honey they have stored, and this has to be weakened with water before it can be fed to larvae. Therefore, in spring many bees can be seen drinking at puddles in roadways, in roof gutters and such places. They carry the water back to the hive in their honey stomachs, in the same way as they carry nectar.

This is not the only time bees need water. The colony keeps the temperature in its nursery very strictly controlled. If it is getting too cold, they increase their movements to warm it, much as we shiver when cold. But if it is getting too hot, they have to prevent overheating. By beating their wings, thus fanning air through the hive, they can keep temperatures down to some extent. If this is not enough, they have to use other means. They carry in water, and place it in the mouths of the cells of the combs. As the water dries off, it cools the comb; if you wet your hand, and blow on it, you will feel this same cooling effect. Dances like those for food may even be done if there is a great need for cooling water.

Bees drinking from puddles

Handling bees

Bees sting, so if you are to handle them you must either be an expert and know how *not* to annoy them, or you must protect yourself. The bee-keeper wears a veil over his face. This veil is a fine mesh of wire or plastic. Although he can see out through it, the bees cannot get in to sting his face. Rapid movement of the eyelids when blinking annoys bees and this is why protection of the eyes is important.

The bee-keeper may also wear gloves to protect his hands. If the gloves are short, the bees may crawl up his sleeves and sting his arms, so it is wise to make a pair of gauntlets or sleeves which cover the gap between gloves and jacket.

Since bees tend to crawl up anything they land on, it is very likely that they will crawl up your leg from the ground. Tuck your trouser legs into your socks to avoid this. Girls should wear slacks tucked into their socks.

Smoke frightens bees and makes them eat their fill from the honey cells in the hive. Then they are much less likely to sting. The bee-keeper carries a little smoke-making machine, and a few puffs from this makes sure the bees fill up with honey and do not bother him.

Contents